CORNELIUS GOES WEST

CHARLIE STEEL

CORNELIUS GOES WEST

CHARLIE STEEL
Tale-Weaver Extraordinaire

Condor Publishing, Inc.
Lincoln, Michigan

CORNELIUS GOES WEST
by Charlie Steel

April 2018

*Cover Illustration by Gail Heath
*Chapter illustrations by Juan Pablo Vega and publishing rights owned by Condor Publishing, Inc.

ISBN-13: 978-1-931079-35-8
Library of Congress Control Number: 2018938893

Condor Publishing, Inc.
PO Box 39
123 S. Barlow Road
Lincoln, MI 48742
www.condorpublishinginc.com

To Joy and Jay

Special People, Special Memories

Chapter 1

Cornelius Kogelschitz hated his name with all the passion his mind could muster. The last name was bad enough but add the first name, Corny, and the teasing he received from other children was just too harsh to endure. He asked his parents where the surname came from but they could not tell him more than it was of German heritage.

"Yours is an honorable name, boy," said his father. "My father and grandfather carried it proudly. You must do the same."

Soon after that conversation, his parents contracted typhus and died.

Corny was saved from the workhouse by his uncle who was married and had eleven children. Even though work took most of their hours and left little time for more than brief morning devotions, the family was close and deeply religious. "Time for blessings," called his uncle as the entire family stumbled in the early morning to prepare to spend long hours toiling in the dirty factories. Everyone stood where they were and bowed their heads as the uncle's voice continued. "Bless us all, dear God, and keep our family safe." After a chorus of Amens, the morning routine continued.

The fourteen of them lived together in the top apartment of a tenement house and every member of that family, adult and child, put in long days at the many factories that choked the area with thick black coal dust and smoke. Food was a luxury, along with water, personal space, and private time. The clothes they wore were seconds and even thirds, and it was up to each member of the family to find soap and wash his or her own in the single kitchen sink. The apartment had a dry sink, and buckets of water had to be hauled up the many floors from the public well on the street below. Such was the life that Cornelius Kogelschitz was rescued into when his parents died.

Had Cornelius the proper food on a daily regimen, he might have grown into a sturdy lad, with greater height and muscle. As it was, food came irregularly and seldom were there any greens or fruit. Often Corny and the other young ones became ill and there was no such thing as a doctor. The mortality rate was high, and many children were taken at all ages. Besides the eleven cousins he now lived with, Corny's aunt had lost several other children to various illnesses. Outbreaks of disease occurred in the slums and close quarters of the tenements and children and adults succumbed like flies. Bodies piled up on the streets along with the garbage. If the government officials hadn't taken prompt action to send carts and workmen down to pick up the corpses, more disease would have spread throughout the city.

It was Sunday, after church, and one of those rare moments when fourteen-year-old Corny could actually relax. Up on the roof of the tenement house, he laid on a brick ledge and daydreamed about a picture he had once seen in a store window. A sign below it had read *Colorado*. There were blue skies with white fleecy clouds, snow-capped mountains, green grass and trees, and a clear rushing stream.

Some day, he thought with grim determination, *I will go there, or a place like it.*

A pigeon flew down to a few bread crumbs, and Corny pulled on a string that jerked the stick holding the box. The container landed heavily over the bird. Even while relaxing, a Kogelschitz must be active or there would be no food to eat for that night's supper. Corny had a long day of it—catching enough birds to feed the many, hungry mouths. All over the city there were countless boys, on thousands of rooftops, doing the same thing. There seemed to be less and less pigeons each year. Sometimes a bird of a different species, like a thrush, would be captured and, despite its meager size, not even it was allowed to escape the pot of a family numbering fourteen.

Still, Corny loved to lie on the roof and absorb a portion of the sun's rays that managed to get through the dirty, smoke-filled skies. Coal dust coated this area of New York City with its black and gray griminess. Everything one touched was instantly stained with soot. Corny was used to it. It dampened his spirit but not his imagination. It was the images in the boy's mind that kept him alive through the drudgery of menial tasks. While he struggled long hours in the textile mills, careful not to lose a limb, he learned to let his imagination soar to places his body could not go. For what did a boy of his circumstances have to look forward to but a wretched life of poverty, hard work, and death?

It was while Corny lay on the roof that he heard the argument between his uncle and aunt.

"It's not enough that we have eleven kids to raise," shouted Louise Kogelschitz. "You just had to bring another mouth to feed under this roof! He's been here for five years and the money he earns isn't enough to feed him! He eats more than two of our children!"

"You exaggerate, Louise," responded Russell Kogelschitz.

"We have to look after our own!" She argued.

"Corny IS of my blood," declared the uncle. "He would have

ended up in the workhouse for children! You know what that place is like."

"Russell, by having that boy here, you are taking the food from our own children's mouths!"

The argument drifted up from an open window directly below. Corny could not hear more of the conversation as the two adults went from the main room into a tiny kitchen. Therefore, the boy on the roof did not hear the conciliatory comments and the conclusion of the argument.

"Louise! I know you're tired, but I won't let you be so harsh. After all, he is a boy and has only us to count on."

"It's the work and the worry that makes me this way, Russell. I'm sorry. May God and you forgive me. Of course, I care for Corny like my own and he will stay with us. After all, he is a good boy."

Corny took the birds he caught that day from a cage and cleaned and butchered them on the roof. He carried the fresh meat down to the apartment and handed them to his aunt who was in the kitchen cooking beans in a large pot.

"Here are some more birds, Aunt Louise," said Corny looking steadily into her face for signs of anger and frustration.

"Oh, thank you," replied the woman with delight. "This will go so well in the pot of beans."

"I guess I will go now, Aunty. Thank you so much for all you've done for me."

"Why, Corny, you're welcome," responded the woman in a quizzical tone. "You go and rest or play, and I'll call you when it's time for supper."

Corny stepped into a small bedroom strewn with mattresses and blankets where the boys slept. In a torn part of his stuffed bedding, he found a tobacco can containing four dollars and twenty-seven cents, all the money he had ever been able to save. He dumped it out and put four one dollar bills in his right shoe. The change he dropped in a front pants pocket, one that did not have a hole in it. Then he took extra underwear, socks, his only other pants and shirt, and laid them flat on his blanket. These he rolled into a tight bundle and tied it with two strings. He fastened a thin cord to the blanket in such a fashion as to make a sling. Corny put on his cap and ragged coat, and slung the blanket bundle around his neck and over one shoulder. Lastly, he bent down and took from a cigar box a long bit of string, two fishing hooks embedded in a bit of cloth, a small magnifying glass, and his most precious possession—a pocket knife with three sharp blades, only one of which was broken. These last items he placed securely in various coat pockets. The youth took one long last look around the little bedroom, and walked quietly out through the living room. He stepped past the kitchen and through the open door of the apartment to the hallway that stank of boiled cabbage. Looking around and seeing no one to question him, he ran down the backstairs to the street below.

In the shadow of the alley, Corny looked up at the apartment building where he had spent the last five years. Even though it was a drab, run-down affair, it had been his home with his only living relatives. His uncle, aunt, and cousins over the years had been very good to him. Despite their circumstances they treated him no differently than a member of their own family. After his parent's death, he felt safe living with his relatives. If he had not heard the conversation between his aunt and uncle, he would never have left, but he was not going to be a burden to anyone. He felt no animosity towards his aunt, only sadness. He was sorry to leave, even fearful of the unknown future, but he would not take food from the mouths of his cousins. Somehow he would get along and make his own way in the world.

It was not until after supper that the two adults agreed that Corny must have heard their argument earlier that afternoon. They checked and found his blanket, clothes, and few possessions gone.

"I would not have the boy think I did not want him," lamented Louise Kogelschitz. "Not for all the food in the world. I just said those things out of anger and frustration. Please let the good Lord and you, husband, forgive me. Poor Corny, out on the streets and it is my doing."

Russell, in response, combed city block after city block late into the night. He returned to the apartment early the next morning without the boy.

Chapter 2

Corny walked a great distance, careful not to make eye contact with suspicious and tough-looking strangers. He hurried on his way, appearing as if he belonged and knew exactly where he was going. The boy found his way to the railroad station and the many tracks leading out of the city. Corny knew enough not to go into the station or anyplace where the railroad bulls might be lurking. If he was to get aboard a freight, he must catch one further down the line. Corny knew there was danger from the wheels of the train, and perhaps even more from the club of the brakeman and the hands of seasoned bums. There was no such thing as a free ride in the life he lived, and what he was about to do involved great risk.

Cornelius Kogelschitz walked down the road near the tracks with a heart full of determination and fear. If he was going to escape New York City, he needed all the courage he could muster. On he walked with his few possessions, looking for a place to make the leap onto a moving train. If he got aboard, he had a chance—a chance to go west and make a new life. To stay meant certain death, for New York City had no place for orphans. Being beaten by gangs, picked up by the police and sent to some unknown place, or freezing and starving to death in an alley was not the way he wanted to die. So he walked on, holding in his mind the lovely vision of Colorado.

Corny found a rise of land with a ledge above the tracks where he could run along the side of the train and jump down. He sat and waited for a freight train to come by. It did not take more than a couple of hours. By then, dusk was turning into blackness. With his heart thumping in his chest, he ran alongside the moving train as fast as his legs could carry him. The clanking wheels and the loud rumbling of the heavy weight of the cars made the ground shake. As the ladder of the car came closer, Cornelius jumped and the blanket bundle nearly tangled up in his hands as he reached for and desperately clutched at the metal rungs. The palms of his hands slapped hard against the steel and they stung. His fingers slipped and then held. The speed of the train twisted his body back sideways, nearly wrenching his hands from his tenuous grip and straining his wrists. It was his feet catching the lower rungs that saved him from losing his grasp and falling. Had he fallen, he certainly would have gone under the wheels to be cut in two.

With aching wrists, the boy held on as the train continued to speed along. Gaining courage, he began to work his way up the ladder. After a time, he climbed up onto the top of the box car. He lay there and rested for a long while.

Worried that a brakeman might find him, he worked himself along the top of the car until he came to a gondola, the kind with no top. Stored in the bottom of the car was metal pipe securely held by tight chains and machinery covered with canvas. Corny found an opening, squeezed in, removed his blanket and used it as a pillow. Cramped, but feeling somewhat safer than before, he relaxed, and after a while finally succumbed to the swaying of the gondola and fell asleep.

Several times during the night he awoke. Once, feeling very stiff and cramped, he crawled out from his hiding place and stretched.

The youth looked up with arms raised and for the first time in his life saw a vast array of twinkling stars. The sight took his breath away and he craned his neck to look in all directions. For long minutes he stared at the multitude of stars he never knew existed. In New York City the sky filled with clouds of dirty soot filled smoke had never been like this. How fresh and clean the air was here in the open countryside, how beautiful was the night sky, filled with millions of tiny pulsing lights.

Afraid of being out in the open, Corny crawled back into his cramped hiding place. He adjusted his blanket, laid his head against the soft material, and listened to the rattling and rumbling of the train. The vibrations he felt were not unpleasant sensations. He tried to sleep but unwanted thoughts flooded his brain—thoughts he tried to push back but without success. He began to dread the worrisome ideas that engulfed him with a fear he had never known before.

What will happen to me? He thought. *Where will this train take me? Will the police find me and lock me up? Will I be put in a workhouse that Uncle Russell and Aunt Louise use to tell me about? Will I be whipped and beaten? Chained or locked in a cell at night? Or will I find work? There are cowboys out west. They ride horses and herd cattle. It would be fun to become a cowboy. How I would like to work outdoors! In that picture of Colorado there were mountains and trees, water, and green grass. It would be wonderful to plant things, to work in the earth, to be around animals.*

As more pleasant thoughts came to Cornelius, he eventually drifted off into a deep sleep.

He awoke to the clatter and movement of the train. It was morning and the sun was above the horizon. Light shined onto the canvas and created flickering shadows. Cornelius sat up quickly and crashed his forehead on part of the machinery. Rubbing his head, he slowly squeezed his stiff body out from the cramped space. He was nearly blinded with bright sunlight. His eyes adjusted and he found himself looking into an azure blue sky. Standing up and peering over the side of the open car, he saw flat plowed fields with neat rows of growing plants. He recognized the low stalks of green corn, nearly knee high, extending across acres and acres of land. There was also wheat and large fields of grass. The train sped past, and the boy could not get enough of staring at the clean open land and blue sky—so different from the dirty, gray, crowded streets of New York City.

By afternoon, Cornelius knew his great mistake. He was so thirsty he could hardly swallow. He should have invested in a canteen and some type of food. How long he could survive without water, he did not know. To jump off the train and later try to get on another, was a desperate idea he did not want to contemplate. He felt that if he tried to board another train, he would surely fall to his death. It was only by luck that he managed to catch the train he was on. Besides, he had a perfect hiding place. Where would he find another?

In the afternoon, rumbles of thunder echoed above the sound of the clattering train. Then it began to rain and water pooled in hollows of the canvas.. The boy eagerly gulped the captured water. Just when his thirst was quenched, the train slowed and stopped. He squeezed back into his hiding place where he remained until the train started moving again. Eventually, with his empty stomach growling for food, he fell asleep.

Cornelius woke to jerking stops and starts. Sometimes he could feel whole cars being shunted off the main body of the train. It was dusk and the boy sipped up the last of the water remaining on the outer surface of the canvas. The water tasted oily and gagged him, but he was thirsty and drank it anyway. Hunger pains kept biting at his stomach. The train speeded on through the dark, and the lad tried his best to return to sleep. The swaying of the freight car helped him, but the clatter and sudden jerks from time to time, did not.

The night finally turned to day and Cornelius extricated himself from the tight fit below the machinery. Groggy and terribly hungry and thirsty, he stood up and leaned against the side of the gondola to look out over the landscape.

Corny felt a heavy, painful blow strike him in the back of his head. The boy's body as well as his mind drifted into complete darkness.

Hours later he awoke to find himself lying face down. Consciousness came slowly and he was confused. He tried to open his eyes and all he saw and felt were sharp cinders, and then the pain came in a nauseating rush. His head ached. Blood had run down and coated over one eye and it would not fully open. His entire body felt like he had been dragged and he could feel the pain of torn skin on his hands, arms, and legs. It hurt to breathe and it felt as if ribs were broken. There was shooting pain in his left lower arm which was twisted back in an odd shape. When he tried to move, it was agony. And when the pain reached a threshold he could no longer stand, blackness blissfully engulfed him.

Chapter 3

Lucille LaBarge trotted her horse along the path beside the railroad tracks. This was the course she always took on her daily ride back to her father's farm. The black she rode shied from the bundle of rags that lay on the great pile of cinders of the railroad bed. Lucy pulled back on the reins and wondered what it was. As she came nearer she saw quite clearly it was a human being, probably a bum, one of those poor fellows she saw riding the trains. Her father warned her that these were tough men, and repeatedly instructed her to stay away. But this fellow was hurt.

Cautiously, Lucy dismounted and came up to the figure. Looking closely, she could see he was poorly dressed. He lay face down and there was blood. One side of his thin face revealed a youth, not much older than she was, probably fourteen or fifteen. She wondered what he was doing on the track. Was the brakeman so cruel that he hit this poor boy and threw him off the train? Her father had told her such stories.

Lucy ran back to the black and grabbed her canteen from the pommel of the saddle. She opened it and went up to the young man and gently poured water across his face. The blood on his head had congealed and streaks of it were dried on his skin. She wondered if she dare move him. Then she heard a groan. He was alive! The boy's head rose a bit from the rough surface.

"Help me," whispered the young man.

Ignoring her father's words, Lucy bent down and gently tried to turn the lad over.

"Please, Miss. Don't move me. It hurts too much."

"I don't know what to do," responded Lucy.

"I'm hurt bad. Help me."

"I'll try," said Lucy, answering the boy's painful whisper. "I'll be back as soon as I can."

Cornelius barely understood the meaning of the words and then the pain was too much and again there was blackness. Lucy saw the young man's eyes close and it appeared that he was again unconscious.

He must be hurt very badly, she thought.

Leaving the canteen at the young man's side, in case he was able to take a drink, she got up and ran to her black. She was so anxious that the horse shied from her. She spoke a few sharp words and the steed calmed and came up to her extended hand. Quickly she mounted, and as she spurred away up the trail, she thought of the closest neighbors.

Wesley and Sandy Mauldin lived on a homestead just a few miles off the trail. They were an older couple. Sandy worked a huge garden and sold vegetables in town. Wesley was a fixer and jack-of-all-trades for the community, and he also shoed horses. These were friends and kind folks, and Lucy was sure they would help. She spurred her black gelding and galloped up the trail to the Mauldin farm.

As she rode, she recalled the young man's thin face. If he had proper clothes, was cleaned up and gained weight, he might be a good looking boy. What she saw of him was a strange green eye, a thick blond eyebrow, and sandy hair. Even injured he had a special presence about him. She wondered why he was riding the rails. He didn't seem to be one of those tough dangerous tramps her father so often warned her about. She hoped she could find help. Strangely, she did not care what her father might say. She would do all she could for the young man. He seemed so weak and helpless, and if he lay there long, he would surely die.

As the girl rode to the front of the Mauldin house, Sandy came out to greet her.

"Hello, Lucy. So long since you've visited."

"Sandy! I need your help—and Wesley's. Is he here?"

"What's happened?"

"A boy—a young man—he's hurt!"

"Where?"

"Two miles east of here, along the rails."

"Wesley!" shouted Sandy. "Wesley!"

Her husband came running from a work shed out back. Lucy explained about the young man she found and just how injured he seemed to be. Without asking further questions, Wesley harnessed two horses to an old work wagon while Sandy and Lucy gathered items they would need. Lucy mounted the black and the Mauldins followed in the wagon. The last part of the trail along the tracks to the injured young man was over very rough ground. The heavy vehicle bounced and swayed and rattled, but Lucy heard no complaints. She was grateful for such friends.

They found him as she had left him. Wesley took a board from the back of the wagon and laid it beside the young man. The three of them carefully turned the injured boy over and onto the wide board. They lifted the groaning but unconscious lad onto the bed of the wagon. There Sandy and Wesley worked on him. The first thing they did was use water to cleanse his injured head and to remove the dried blood. Under their ministrations Cornelius gained consciousness.

"It hurts," moaned the lad.

"Sorry," answered Wesley. "Tell us what pains the most."

"My arm."

"Yes, and what else?" asked Wesley gently.

"It hurts to breathe!"

"Anything else?"

"My head. Something hit my head. I must have fallen from the train."

"I think, lad," said Sandy softly, "that one of the guards hit you and threw you off. You're in good hands now."

Cornelius lifted his head and tried to focus his eyes. All he saw were blurry figures and then the pain was too much. He fell again into unconsciousness.

"Good," commented Wesley. "Now that he's out, we'll straighten his arm and put on splints. Then we'll take him home. The ride over the rough ground will surely hurt him, better he can't feel it."

Lucy watched as Wesley gently touched and examined the boy's lower arm. Wesley and Sandy were often called upon when people were sick since the doctor was far away. Sandy helped hold up the arm and then Wesley laid it across the rail of the wagon. Grasping it firmly, he pushed down with sudden force. There was the sound of crunching bone. When the arm was gently laid down for the splints, it looked straight again. After setting it, they bandaged his head wound.

This time Lucy followed behind the wagon and watched the blanketed young man. Wesley tried to guide the conveyance carefully over the bumps but repeatedly it lurched and rattled over uneven ground. The young man, even in unconsciousness, called out in pain. Slowly they made the two miles back to the farm and all three helped carry the boy into the house and to the spare bedroom.

"You sit in the kitchen and have a cup of coffee, Lucy," instructed Sandy. "We'll attend to the lad."

"Is there anything you can do for his pain?"

"We have laudanum, but we need to see how bad his head injury is," interjected Wesley. "Don't want to put him too far to sleep until we know."

Lucy went to the kitchen and poured herself a cup of coffee. She was too anxious to sit so she stared out through a window and looked at the neat rows of vegetables that were planted over many acres. It wasn't long before Sandy returned.

"Wesley gave him a bit of the laudanum. He is in a great deal of pain, and rest is what he needs. Poor lad is all skin and bones. It looks like he has never had enough to eat. If he gets stronger, we can take care of that."

"If?"

"I'm sorry, Lucy. Some things can only be left to God."

"My father will be so angry once he finds out about this. He goes crazy when he talks about the tramps riding the trains. I'm not to go near them."

"Then we won't tell him, Lucy. It will be between the three of us. Wesley and I will say we found him and, it's true, we did find him."

"Thank you. When he's better, can I come and visit?"

"Of course. Everyday, if you wish. But, I'm afraid it will be some time before we know anything. You see, Lucy, it's not just his head injury, or his broken bones, the poor lad is nearly starved to death."

"Oh!"

"I suspect from his clothes, he's from some big city."

"Is there anything I can do? I have a little savings. Would that help?"

"Well, Lucy," said Sandy. "We have plenty of food. It would take two of that boy to fit into Wesley's clothes. If Wesley had a little money, he could go to the general store near Westport and get the lad a new outfit."

"I'll bring it tomorrow!"

"Not so fast," replied Sandy. "It will be some time before he will be up and able to get dressed."

Wesley came into the kitchen and poured himself coffee and sat down. He, too, thought the boy had ridden the rails from a large city. At this point Lucy looked at a little watch she carried on a gold chain around her neck and saw that it was late. She said her goodbyes to the Mauldins and thanked them for their help.

"I think," said Wesley as he watched the girl ride away. "That Lucy has more than a casual interest."

"Yes, husband. That goes without question. But, what about us? Can we afford to keep the boy?"

"I won't be turning out a starving, helpless lad."

"Of course not, but what about…after?"

"We don't even know if he's going to survive. If he lives, we always have plenty of food."

"We'll see, Wesley," said Sandy. "We'll see."

Chapter 4

Claude LaBarge waited in front of the big house. For once he was not looking at his thousands of acres of richly irrigated fields. He was worried, and that worry erupted with fury. Where was she? Then the father saw her approach.

"Daughter!" He shouted to the girl on the black horse. "Where have you been?"

"Riding."

"Do you know what time it is?"

"Yes, a little after six."

"And what time are you to be here?"

"No later than five o'clock."

"Yes! And you had me worried sick. This is what I get for raising a girl on my own."

"But, Father! I love to ride!"

"Love to, nothing! I have people watching and was told which direction you rode. And when you do ride again, you will stay away from the railroad tracks, or I will sell Blacky! You're not to ride the rest of the week!"

"That's not fair!"

"I mean it, daughter. Now take Blacky down to the stables and hurry back for supper. And be prepared to tell me exactly what happened that made you so late."

When Lucy returned to the house and the dining room, the maid served supper. Lucy told some of the story of seeing the Mauldins find an injured boy along the tracks. She explained how she stopped to help.

"Daughter! How many times have I told you not to go near strangers?"

"But I was not alone, Father," lied Lucy.

"These tramps can carry terrible diseases and you are not immune. You will obey me. No more riding for a week!"

"But, Father, how will I know how the boy is?"

"Are you saying this to make me angrier? I forbid you to go to the Mauldins or to see that boy under any circumstances! Am I understood?"

"Yes, Father."

"Now promise me you will do as I say." There was a long silence as the father stared at the top of his daughter's head. "Well?"

Lucy crossed her fingers on both hands below the table and then answered.

"I promise, Father."

Chapter 5

Cornelius Kogelschitz's condition worsened over the next several days, and Sandy and Wesley Mauldin were not sure if their young patient would recover. The combination of the severe head wound, broken ribs and arm, and lacerated skin caused extreme pain to the starved youth. The Mauldins fretted over the boy. They did all they could for the lad, and he was too sick to take more than a little broth into his empty stomach. Still Sandy and Wesley did their best. Twenty-four hours a day there was always one of them in the room watching over him.

The young man developed a fever which worsened. All they could do was offer cold compresses and try to keep his body cool. Sandy talked to the boy and, when she ran out of conversation, she read to him. She selected *The Sketch-Book* written in the pen name of Geoffrey Crayon, Gent. Sandy explained to the lad that the book was really written by a famous writer named Washington Irving. In his book he was expressing sympathy for the way the American Indians were treated and their lands stolen. Sandy noticed that if she read to him, the youth's restlessness eased. She was not certain this poor unfortunate lad understood; nevertheless, she continued to plow through the entire book and the boy seemed to relax with the spoken words. However, Sandy thrilled to note that the young man was especially alert when she read the tale of *Rip Van Winkle.*

The days passed, but the boy did not improve. He was sweating his life away in high fever. When delirious he would talk and often it was something about his family. Several times the lad shouted out for his mother and in the sick room they heard grief expressed once again as the young man relived her fevered death.

"Mother, please, you must get well. I love you, Mama. Please, please, please don't die," he would cry over and over again.

Sometimes his fevered cries lasted for hours. There were other instances where the youth talked of family, of work in the factory, of grief and loneliness that came from a life lived in the slums of New York City.

One day Wesley came into his room and expressed concern to his wife. She was reading over the sick lad.

"I'm afraid for him. We have done all we can yet his fever is getting worse. If the boy hadn't been starved when he came to us, I'm sure he would have recovered by now. But he is weak and getting weaker."

"What more can be done, Wesley?" asked Sandy in a subdued voice.

"I saw an Indian do this with a child," he answered, picking up the young man in his strong arms. "Follow me."

Wesley Mauldin carried the lad out to the shed where he stabled the horses. In front was a pump and below it a wooden water trough. It was full of fresh cold water, and into this, the young man was gently immersed. Wesley carefully held his neck, head, and shoulders. For several minutes the boy's body lay under the cool water, and both Sandy and Wesley could see the bright redness fade to a gray white cast.

"Will he catch lung fever, Wesley?"

"We have no choice. He will die anyway if we don't do something."

"At least the red has gone from his face."

"Perhaps we will have to do this several times."

It was just as Wesley stated. After drying the boy and returning him to the covers of the bed, he slept more peaceably and his fever left him for several hours. Each time he turned red and perspired, they dunked him in the cool water. After each immersion, they were able to get warm broth and water into him. In this manner, the fever finally broke and the lad had a long peaceful sleep. When he awoke on the fifth day, he was lucid, full of questions, and ravenously hungry.

At the end of the week, Lucy came to visit. She told the Mauldins she had an argument with her father over finding the young man. Knowing Lucy's determination and what her visits could mean to the boy, the Mauldins agreed to keep the visit a secret. Sandy warned her that her father eventually would have to be told.

"I am old enough to make my own decisions," Lucy argued. "Father had no right to forbid me to come here!"

Sandy merely smiled and then told Lucy the boy's name.

"Cornelius Kogelschitz? Oh, how unusual! I bet they call him Corny."

Lucy handed Sandy fifteen dollars.

"I hope," whispered the girl. "That will be enough; it's all I have."

"More than enough to buy him new clothes," replied Sandy, stashing the money away.

"From what Wesley said, you had a difficult week," Lucy stated. "I wish I could have been here."

"Yes, he was very weak and it was a close call.

“I’m so glad he didn’t die.”

“Do you want to go in and talk to Cornelius?”

“Could I? I mean, ah, would it be all right?”

“Yes, of course. I already told him about you and that you would be coming by. He said he wanted to meet the person who found him.”

“What do I say?” asked Lucy breathlessly.

“Why, say hello, and whatever else comes into your mind. Wait here and I’ll see if he’s awake.”

Sandy Mauldin smiled to herself. She felt as if she were party to a secret meeting and that this could be the beginning of a fortuitous friendship. Knowing how the girl’s father felt, made the older woman reflect on what she was doing. For a moment she hesitated. Then she thought, *After all, Lucy found the boy, and has certainly saved his life.*

“Cornelius!” called Sandy Mauldin. “Lucy LaBarge is here. The girl who found you.”

“Mrs. Mauldin, can you help me sit up?”

Sandy helped the young man rise and she piled extra pillows behind his head. She pulled up the sheet and covers, and then folded them back neatly over his waist.

“Cornelius!” corrected the woman. “How many times have I told you to call me Sandy?”

“I, I just can’t, Mrs. Mauldin. My aunt, and before that my mother, taught me never to call an adult by their given name—unless they were part of the family.”

“And you don’t consider us family?”

“No disrespect, Mrs. Mauldin. This is—this is all so sudden.”

“Then call me Aunt Sandy. Can you do that?”

“Yes Mrs., ah, Aunt Sandy.”

“That’s better, now I’ll ask Lucy in.”

“Please Mrs. Mauldin, what do I say?

“Why, just say hello!” and then the woman smiled all the way out of the sick room.

Shyly, Lucy LaBarge stepped into the bedroom. Her amber eyes were big and round and her face, despite herself, betrayed her emotions. She turned deep red, and the flush continued up to her forehead. She could even feel her ears burning with the rise of her own hot blood. She had her eyes to the floor and became angry with herself. Confused by her strange reactions, she stomped her foot and raised her vision to encompass the room and the figure lying in the bed.

“Hello,” they both said at the same time.

Lucy noted that Cornelius’s face seemed to turn a deeper crimson. Was it a lingering fever due to his illness, or was he also embarrassed and uncomfortable?

“I am so glad you are better,” Lucy said, staring at him.

She noted his sandy blond hair combed over a straight forehead. Except for the scabs, his thin face was smooth and clean. He stared back at her with intense green eyes.

“Yes, I am,” answered Cornelius. “I was told it was you who found and saved me.”

“Oh no, I only found you. It was the Mauldins who did everything else.”

“They said you helped carry me.”

“Well, yes. But that was nothing.”

“It was very brave of you to help a stranger.”

“What else could I do?”

“Still, thank you for what you did.”

There was a long silence between the girl and the boy. They did not break eye contact. Both of their faces retained the red stain.

"The Mauldins told me your name. Corny, isn't it?"

There was a short gasp from the girl and she covered her mouth with her hand. Suddenly the two of them were laughing. When the laugh ended the red in their faces had disappeared.

"Pretty corny name, isn't it?" The boy asked with a grin.

"You could change it," commented Lucy.

"My parents gave it to me, I would never change it. It's all I have now that they are gone."

"Oh, I'm so sorry. I understand."

"It's all right, Lucy. My parents died more than five years ago."

"I meant no offense, Cornelius."

"Call me Corny."

The youth smiled at the girl and there was a long, awkward silence.

"Where are you from?" asked Lucy, sitting down in a wooden chair beside the lad's bed.

Cornelius found himself telling her part of his life's story.

"You see, no matter how hard I worked in the factory, they paid so little, and I was an extra person to feed. I couldn't take food out of the mouths of my cousins, so I decided to leave."

He told her about getting aboard the train and the long ride. He was still not clear how he ended up on the railroad bed where she found him.

"I'm sorry; I didn't mean to talk so much." Cornelius declared.

"Don't be. It was interesting. I couldn't do what you did. I would be too frightened."

"I don't think you would be frightened at all," he replied.

"But you were brave to face the world on your own."

"When you have no choice in the matter, it is very easy to be scared and brave at the same time."

"I'll remember that," she said. "I'm so glad I found you and you are going to be okay."

"You're very kind," Cornelius blurted out. "You are the first girl I have ever spoken to other than my cousins."

"And, you are the first boy," she answered.

"Why? Surely you have many friends."

"No. My father is very strict and doesn't let me talk to anyone outside of school—and there are only two boys my age in my class—the McIver bullies. I stay away from them. Anyway, when I told father about you, he forbade me to come here and see you."

"I don't understand. Then why did you come?"

"Because, I had to find out if you were well. And, my father is too strict. He had no right to..."

"At least you have a father. He must love you very much."

Lucy stomped her foot in sudden anger.

"I won't be told what to do by anyone. This time he's wrong."

"You mustn't defy your father, Lucy."

There was another long pause and then Cornelius chose his words carefully.

"I didn't mean to upset you, Lucy. You found me and got help; otherwise I wouldn't be alive. But now that you know I'm all right, you don't need to get in more trouble with your father over someone like me."

"What does that mean?"

"It means that I know what your father is thinking and it's true. I am nothing but an orphan. Not someone you should be friends with."

"I'll choose my own friends, thank you! If I want to ride Blacky, I will. And if I want to come over here and visit, I will. And besides,

Sandy and Wesley have been my friends for a long time. Father knows that. He has no right to forbid it, or to take my riding away from me—the one thing I love."

"Blacky is your horse?"

"Yes. He's magnificent and all mine. He's part thoroughbred and Morgan, and he can run like the wind."

The two were so absorbed in their conversation they didn't notice Sandy Mauldin entering with a tray. On it was a bowl of steaming hot chicken soup.

"Excuse me," interrupted Sandy. "I am glad to see the two of you getting along. Lucy, I'm sorry but Cornelius has been up quite a while now and he must eat his lunch and then rest."

"All right, Sandy."

"You can come back tomorrow and visit."

"Lucy said her father told her not to come here, Mrs. Mauldin," said Cornelius. "She shouldn't, if it will get her in trouble."

"Did you tell him that, Lucy?" asked Sandy.

"Yes, I did. I didn't mean to tell him. It just came out."

"Well, that is a matter Lucy will have to work out with her father," said Sandy.

"She should obey him," said Cornelius.

"If I want to come here, I will," responded Lucy angrily. "I'm going now!"

The young girl, her face flaring red with anger, turned and ran out of the room. Sandy and Corny heard her hurried footsteps, the opening and slamming of the front door, and then the sudden galloping of horse's hooves.

"Well," smiled Sandy. "I see the two of you are off to an interesting friendship."

"Mrs. Mauldin." The boy stopped short as Sandy raised her eyebrows and gave a pretend frown. "I mean, Aunt Sandy, I didn't mean to make her angry, but I don't want her to be in trouble with her father."

"I know, Cornelius. But, if it wasn't you, sooner or later it certainly would be someone else. Now you eat your soup and rest."

Cornelius ate and Sandy watched him. It was evident his thoughts were far way. It was not hard for the older woman to determine where. She tucked him in, and he went immediately to sleep.

Sandy remained in the room for some time and watched the boy. What a nice young man he seemed to be. She had been afraid at first of becoming too attached; worried that this lad might bring trouble or be of bad character. She had prayed earnestly for God to help in saving the young man's life, and she believed her prayers were answered. Her previous reservations about the youth disappeared. This was not a tough young man; he was no danger to them or the farm. It seemed he would fit in well, and in a way, the lad brought her and her husband Wesley even closer together. Somehow, if possible, the young man's presence gave them a more meaningful existence. Sandy decided that she welcomed Cornelius Kogelschitz with her whole heart, for with his coming he brought a fulfillment the childless couple had been missing.

Chapter 6

With a healthy diet, Cornelius grew stronger, taller, and gained weight. He thrived under Sandy's care. Wesley had taken Lucy's gift of money and traveled to Westport. When Corny left his sick bed he had new store bought clothes and boots.

Cornelius insisted on helping out around the farm. He felt a bond with the older couple, a closeness that matched what he thought he had during the earlier times with Uncle Russell, Aunt Louise, Benny, and his other ten cousins. After all, the Mauldins had taken him in, fed and cared for him, and saved his life. Who wouldn't be grateful under such circumstances?

Wearing his broken arm in a sling, he used the other to carry and fetch. He worked all day with the Mauldins and they enjoyed each other's company. Lucy, in spite of her father, visited frequently. She helped around the farm and the friendship between Lucy and Cornelius grew.

When his arm was fully healed and the sling came off, Cornelius worked even harder. Under the sun, his skin turned nut brown. Muscles began to form on the youth and he filled out further. The young man was quick to learn. He put his energy into his work, and the Mauldins would often tell him to slow down.

"You can't finish it all in one day, Corny," Wesley would exclaim. "That's enough work for today."

This was so much different than working in a dirty factory. Under blue skies the boy tended the huge vegetable fields and cut and bundled hay. He hauled water and feed for the livestock. Corny discovered that he liked working outdoors, and was even better at it than he imagined. In the morning when he awoke, he met each new day with great enthusiasm. Such exuberance was new to him and he exulted in being alive.

How different and wonderful it is out here, thought Corny. *The air is filled with the fragrance of growing grass, flowers, and the sweet earth. When it rains, the odor is not of sulfur and soot, but has a fresh pleasant smell. It is so different from the dirty streets, the cramped and foul smelling buildings. How sad that the rest of my family has to live in a place like that.*

Corny thanked God daily for his deliverance. If anything, his new life gave him more faith. All day long, while working and using his muscles, he would have a running dialogue, a one way mental prayer, with his maker. He prayed for blessings on the harvest, for the Mauldins, Lucy, and his uncle, aunt, Benny, and all the other cousins.

At the end of the day, after long hours spent working in the fields, as tired as he was, Corny never went to supper without a smile on his face. Rather than being upset with the aches and pains his newly acquired muscles gave him, he was truly glad to be working in fresh air. Here the work was natural and it made him feel as if he belonged.

Corny hoped that the Mauldins understood how grateful he was and he tried his best to show it in the work he performed for them. He wanted more than anything to make them proud of him.

The young man did fit in well. At night, they prepared and ate large suppers. They would light the kerosene lamp, finish the dishes, and sit down to talk and play cards. Sometimes Corny told about his past life. The Mauldins encouraged him. He told them that his cousin Benny was his closest and only friend before coming west. Corny expressed concern about how his cousin and closest relatives were faring. The story of New York City, of smoke filled skies and factories, was a bleak picture for the westerners. When Corny described in detail the small, high rent slum apartment, they found it almost unbelievable. The youth explained how he and his cousins were forced to work long hours, for little pay, in laundries and factories. Despite the hard work by all members of the Kogelschitz family, they were unable to afford sufficient food or clothing. The Mauldins listened intently to the young man's story.

One night, after Corny spoke of his family, Sandy made a suggestion.

"Cornelius, it sounds like your aunt and uncle are good, God-fearing people who truly do care for you. People sometimes say things in haste they don't mean. Why don't you write and let them know you are alive and made it safely out west. I know they must be terribly worried about you."

Corny was eager to do so and, with Sandy's help, he sat down to write immediately. When the letter was finished and ready to send, he made sure to enclose money for the Kogelschitz's return postage.

Letters were a rare thing and it took many weeks before a response arrived. One day a neighbor coming from town stopped to deliver mail. The envelope had a New York address. Wesley, Sandy, and Cornelius ended their work early and went into the house to have coffee while the letter was read.

"I can't read very well," admitted the young man.

"That's not a problem," responded Sandy. "I can help you."

Corny took his jackknife and very carefully cut open one edge of the envelope and held the precious letter before him.

"Aunt Louise is the one who can write the best; she had schooling." added Corny.

September 23, 1868
Dear Cornelius,

When we received your letter we were so happy. I cried while reading it to the family and I am afraid I made the ink run. For the first time in our marriage your Uncle Russell was speechless. The children sat down on the floor and listened without making a sound.

Dear sweet Cornelius, to this very day I have regretted with all my heart what you overheard me say on the day you left. I am sorry and would do anything to take my words back.

We are happy to hear you are alive and well. Your uncle and I and the children have read your letter over and over. I fear the paper is going to fall apart. Sandy and Wesley Mauldin sound like good people and we are glad that God led you into their hands. Their farm and the Missouri countryside sounds like a bit of heaven. Your description of the green fields, the open blue sky, and your work on the farm seems wonderful. It is far different than the life you left.

We are very sorry to hear of your injuries but are glad you are well now. We have prayed for your safety since the day you left us. We thank God that our prayers have been answered. Your letter was heaven sent.

Please give our kind regards to the Mauldins. We wish you the best.

In loving kindness,

Louise & Russell Kogelschitz & Family

Tears running down his cheeks, Cornelius set the precious letter down. It was a long time before anyone said anything.

"Your aunt wrote a beautiful response," said Sandy. "Now you know she has only the best wishes and thoughts for you."

"Yes, Aunt Sandy. I'm so glad you suggested I write to them."

The Mauldins spent several days working out a plan. One night, Sandy began speaking of homesteading and how they had proved up on their one-hundred-sixty acres of land, and how they now held a patent. That evening they discussed the Homestead Act. They also gave Corny a copy.

"I tried to read the act you gave me, Aunt Sandy," commented Cornelius a day later. "But I don't understand it."

"Show me and we can try to figure it out together."

"It's this part," Cornelius said and began to read out loud. *Be entitled to enter one quarter section or a less quantity of unappropriated public lands, upon which said person may have filed a preemption claim.* "It doesn't make sense."

"We don't understand all that highfalutin language ourselves!" laughed Wesley.

"How do you file then?" asked Cornelius seriously.

"All you need to know, son," answered Wesley. "Is that you have to be twenty-one, pay a filing fee of ten dollars, a two dollar commission to the land agent, and prove up on the land for five years. You do that by building and farming. After the five years are up, you fill out the "proof" document and pay a final six dollar form fee."

"I have to be twenty-one?" asked Cornelius indignantly.

"Yes, I'm sorry. But that's what it says," Sandy answered him.

"That's seven years from now," responded Cornelius counting

it out on his fingers. "No, wait, I forgot, I'll be fifteen tomorrow, so that'll be six years. Still too long."

"Six years will go by faster than you think," commented Wesley.

"All the good land will be taken up by then!"

"Out here on the prairie you have to have water to make a real success of it," said Wesley. "I'm afraid the dry farmers in the drought years won't make it. Most of the homesteads are along the rivers for that reason, but I know of some tracks of land nearby that have good flowing wells. If you had relatives you could trust, they could come out and file on land with water.

"I trust my uncle and my cousins!" exclaimed Cornelius.

"Of course, you do," said Sandy and she smiled directly at her husband.

"I have a friend who could file on a quarter section for you while it's being proved up and sell it back to you for a low fee," said Wesley. "I've already asked and he said yes. We could work together to farm it, and build a house. Wouldn't that be a way to homestead it now, before it's too late?"

"Would you do such a thing for me?" asked Cornelius, his green eyes staring intently.

"What are friends and relatives for, if not to help each other?"

"Gosh!" exclaimed Cornelius. "My Uncle Russell could file on a one-sixty, and his son, Benny, is turning twenty-one—he could too. If your friend filed for me, that would be one-hundred-sixty acres times three…"

"Four hundred and eighty acres," Sandy explained.

"Uncle Russell, Aunt Louise, and Cousin Benny won't believe this! Four hundred and eighty acres! With water for irrigation we could farm, raise chickens and pigs, and horses and cattle."

"If a person works hard and plans well, and is willing to learn, anything is possible," replied Wesley.

"But how do we get Uncle Russell and his family out here? And how do we pay for the filing fees?"

"You sit down and write to your uncle and his family about this. If they agree, with all of us working and saving, we'll find a way," answered Sandy.

Together, after dinner, the three sat at the kitchen table. Each contributed to the long letter they composed to the Kogelschitz family. That night the two Mauldins sat up in bed. They discussed quietly what young Cornelius Kogelschitz meant to their lives.

"His coming to us has been a blessing," whispered Sandy to Wesley.

Chapter 7

The next day Lucy came early for the surprise birthday party for Cornelius. She traveled with Wesley to Westport to purchase gifts. He told her about the plan to bring Cornelius's family to Missouri to homestead.

"Oh, how exciting!" expressed Lucy, and she beamed a smile at Wesley.

While they were gone, Cornelius was kept busy cleaning the horse shed and piling hay into a high bale. Sandy stayed home and baked a cake. That evening, after Cornelius had washed up, he entered the house. Lucy led the Mauldins and several visiting neighbors in wishing him a happy birthday.

Lucy's gift to her fifteen-year-old friend was a leather jacket. It was an expensive one, a kind he or the Mauldins could never afford. It was fancy, with fringe and Indian designs, and lined on the inside. The two youths sat and talked and ate cake and drank cider while more visitors arrived. Several of the neighbors brought instruments and they began to fiddle and play the banjo. Despite the word getting out late, more neighbors came with food. Tables were brought out and set up, and the party spilled out into the yard.

At dusk Wesley sought help to find, light, and hang all the lanterns he owned. Cornelius and Lucy had their very first dance. Like all such parties, once begun, the hard-working neighbors were reluctant to leave. The music and dancing ran past midnight before it ended and people started for home.

As some of the lanterns burned out, Lucy and Corny found themselves alone in the dark. It was quite late. Corny knew his comment would upset her but he made his suggestion anyway.

"Lucy, don't you think you should go home now? It's late and your father…"

"Trying to get rid of me, are you?" teased Lucy.

"No. You know better than that. I never had a birthday party before and this evening has been so exciting. Some of the neighbors brought gifts of food and I never even met them before. That coat you gave, it's much too nice for the likes of me. But most of all, it was very pleasant to dance with you, to hear music, to talk…"

"Yes?"

"It's always so nice to be in your company," said Corny, seriously and with unusual formality.

Lucy laughed.

"And for me to be in yours, kind sir," replied Lucy, laughing once more.

"I didn't mean it as a joke," replied Cornelius.

"I didn't take it as that," replied Lucy. "We are great friends, aren't we? I bet there isn't one thing I don't know about you, or you don't know about me. That's what friends are for? To share their secrets, their thoughts, their…"

"Troubles?" said Cornelius, completing the sentence for her.

"Yes," said Lucy.

"I'm glad you're my friend. I think of you often when I'm working in the fields. Sometimes I talk to God about you."

"You do?"

Chapter 8

Nearly an hour later, as Lucy entered the courtyard, her father, Claude LaBarge, had the house, the barn, and the stables lit with lanterns. Men and horses were everywhere. The furious owner shouted orders. No speculation was needed on Lucy's part—she was in great trouble. The farm hands came running forward and at the head of them was her father, his face purple with rage.

"Where have you been, young lady?"

"I'm sorry, Father; I was at the Mauldin's."

"What's that you say?"

"The Mauldins had a birthday party for Cornelius and I attended it. Didn't you get my note on the mantel? You were invited, too. There was dancing and dinner. Everyone was there. I wanted you to meet Cornelius and see that he is not at all like you believe."

Lucy saw that her father was so angry he began to choke. Whatever words he was trying to say, wouldn't come out. All she heard was a gasping sound. This was followed by a deep growl. After some coughing and clearing of his throat, the man managed to talk.

"Lucy!" he bellowed. "I ignored the invitation, and I was certain you did too. And, no, I didn't find your note. How dare you go! After I forbade you and you promised!"

"That was a long time ago, Father. I'm nearly fifteen now. Besides, everyone knows the Mauldins and Cornelius are good and hard-working folks. Why didn't you come to the party? You would have found me there."

"This is an outrage! How dare you sit up on that horse and talk to me like this!"

"Father, you're making a spectacle of yourself."

"Enough!" He yelled and turned to the workmen. "You men, call off the search. Lucy, you get off that horse. I'll take charge of it personally."

"I'll stay on Blacky until you calm down."

"Girl! Where did you learn such insolence? From that tramp you met?"

"Cornelius is no tramp. You shout and yell, but you never listen. Will you please be reasonable?"

"Be reasonable? When you defy my orders and stay out all night? Do you have any idea what you put me through? Not to mention those who live and work on this farm?"

"Will you please stop shouting?"

"No, daughter. Enough is enough. I am taking Blacky and selling him tomorrow. If I can't sell him, I'll ship him far away. Tonight is the last night you will ever go riding by yourself."

"You wouldn't!"

"Yes, I would and I will! Now get off that horse and go to your room. You stay there until I say otherwise. In fact, I'm going to lock you in until you learn how to behave."

"No, Father."

"No?"

"I'm not a child. You never listen to me or try to understand. You just yell and give orders. I hate it, and I'm not going to live like this any longer."

"Lucy!"

"You heard me. The Mauldins treat me better than you do. They are loving, and kind..."

Claude LaBarge's face turned into an angry purple mask of rage, and he stepped forward to grab the reins of the black horse. Blacky snorted in fear and rose up on hind legs. The black came down several feet distant and Lucy's father came forward again. Again the horse reared up.

"Please, don't scare Blacky."

"Daughter! If you don't get down off that horse now, I'm not responsible for what happens next!"

"Daddy, please! Won't you calm down and listen to me, just for once?"

"Never! Now get off that horse! When I catch him, this will be the last you will ever see of him."

"Father! You gave me Blacky. You said he was mine forever."

"That was before you defied me!"

"All right then. If that's the way you want it."

"What are you doing, daughter?"

"Leaving!"

"Don't you dare!"

"I tried to please you—I really did. I won't live here like this anymore."

Her father lunged one more time for the reins and Blacky snorted. Lucy pulled sharply back, and the bit tore at the animal's sensitive mouth. Again the black backed up and then rose high on its hind hooves. Lucy spurred the horse; it screamed in pain and then jumped into a long leap. It came down heavily on all fours, and again Lucy spurred. The enraged animal snorted, leaped forward, and continued into a running gallop to quickly disappear into the darkness.

Claude LaBarge looked out into the inky blackness and the furious rage slowly left him. There was a hollow sickening feeling in his stomach. His head ached, and his heart thumped heavily. A deep remorse for his violent behavior welled up in him and he stifled a cry. *What have I done?* he thought. *In the state she and the horse are in, anything can happen.*

LaBarge knew that in places the ground was rough, and in the dark the horse and girl could fall and she may become injured or worse. This was the first time Lucy had ever defied him so. He would take a saddled horse and go after her. He would have the men follow. But this time, when he caught up to her, he would not yell. He would try to stay calm, and for the first time in his life he would really listen.

Father and hands searched all night. Daylight came and still there was no Lucy. Claude LaBarge personally covered vast distances in the direction she had taken. He followed tracks west—towards the Missouri River. Why would she have gone that way if she was so fond of the Mauldins and that boy she talked about? Was she so upset that she spurred her horse in malice in the opposite direction?

By noon LaBarge admitted defeat and turned back to his farm. There he bathed and changed clothing. He called for his foreman. They discussed trackers and agreed to find and hire Blue, a local Fox Indian. LaBarge told his foreman to pay the Indian anything he demanded, as long as he would search for his daughter. Orders were given for the workmen to continue looking for Lucy, while he went to the Mauldins to see if she had returned there.

Chapter 9

It was Cornelius who saw the big man on a dark Morgan ride into the yard. There was a faint resemblance between the father and daughter. What made Corny sure this was Lucy's father was the manner in which he acted. The look of authority and anger were chiseled into his features. He carried himself as a man in charge and someone not to be trifled with. He dismounted, pointed his finger, and demanded.

"Where is my daughter?"

"Lucy?" asked Cornelius.

"Is there another girl who visits here?"

"No sir. Lucy isn't here. Is something wrong?"

Sandy came out of the house and walked up behind Corny. Wesley was shoeing horses. When he looked up and saw the angry neighbor, he came quickly to stand beside his wife.

"Hello, Mister LaBarge," called Wesley. "Is something wrong?"

"Lucy was here last night," stated the dark-haired man.

"She was," answered Sandy. "She's safe, isn't she? Didn't she get home last night?"

"Yes. It was late, we argued, and she took the black and galloped off. I was hoping she came here."

"No, sir. She didn't come back," replied the young man.

"Are you the one she calls Cornelius?"

"Yes, sir, I am."

"You wouldn't lie to me about Lucy's whereabouts, would you?"

"No, sir."

"I was afraid of that," answered the big man, then his body slumped in obvious exhaustion.

"What's wrong?" asked Wesley. "Did something happen to her?"

"I don't know; I fear the worst. We had an awful argument. Lucy was very upset, and so was her horse. Anything could have happened."

"Of course you have searched for her." Sandy said quietly.

"Yes. I tried to follow her tracks, but I lost them. They led west towards the river. I have my men looking, and I sent my foreman for Blue, the tracker."

"What can we do?" asked Wesley.

"I have tried everything; I don't know what more can be done."

"Come in the house for a cup of coffee," offered Sandy.

The big man sat at the table, head erect, but with visible strain. It was evident he was very tired. Whatever took place the night before between father and daughter greatly affected the land owner. His commanding demeanor could not hide what he was really feeling. Coffee was put before him, and he drank it automatically.

"Mister LaBarge," began Wesley politely. "We care for Lucy a great deal. We will do anything you ask."

"Thank you. She told me you were kind people. She complained that I never really listened to her. That's what the argument was about."

"Don't give up hope, Mister LaBarge," answered Wesley in return.

"I am very afraid for her," replied the big man despondently.

"Contrary to what you may think, I love my daughter. If something has happened to her, I will never forgive myself."

"Cornelius," said Wesley. "Saddle the dun, and hitch up the wagon. Be sure to strap on that old .36 revolver I gave you for your birthday."

Wesley Mauldin turned to the girl's father.

"Mister LaBarge, you're exhausted. You can tell us where to find Lucy's tracks and we'll search. You stay here and rest."

"No, I will go with you."

"Then let me ride your horse; you can rest in the wagon. Sandy will drive you over to your ranch while Cornelius and I follow Lucy's trail."

"But I sent my foreman for the Indian."

"There's no way of knowing if your foreman found the tracker. There's no time to waste."

"What makes you think you can find Lucy when we couldn't?"

"You're tired, sir. The more people searching, the better the chances. Besides, the three of us care for Lucy. We won't give up until she's found."

"Thank you, Mauldin. It's more than I deserve."

"Sandy," directed Wesley. "You get blankets so Mr. LaBarge can try to sleep in the back of the wagon. Cornelius and I will leave now. You watch for our tracks and follow as best you can."

Cornelius returned with the harnessed wagon. Tied behind was the saddled dun.

"Come on, Corny. You take the dun. I'm riding Mister LaBarge's horse. We'll go ahead."

"Wesley," called LaBarge. "You'll pick up her tracks going west from the front yard of my home. You can't miss them. If you find her, I'll never forget it."

"Don't you worry, sir," responded Wesley. "We'll keep going until we do."

Cornelius was not quite used to the saddle but he followed behind Wesley as best he could. He was worried about Lucy and this was no time to complain about saddle sores. Wesley had done some trapping and he knew how to read sign. They picked up the deep impressions of Lucy's horse and followed them west. Most of the time Wesley could follow from the saddle, and they moved swiftly. But when they hit firm ground, he dismounted and worked out the trail. He intently followed the tracks and they covered much ground. As they moved forward, the older man scratched arrows in the dirt or left trail markers for Sandy to follow in the wagon.

"She was riding recklessly all this way," commented Wesley. "She must have been quite upset to spur the horse like that through the dark."

Cornelius didn't respond and they kept going. They came to the Missouri River and split up.

"She rode the horse in the water. No telling which way she came out. Corny, you take the river north; I'll follow south. If you find her, fire that revolver of yours three times. If I find her, I'll do the same."

Cornelius thumped his heels against the dun gelding's sides and reined the horse north along the shore of the great river. Riding over the rough ground, he took a pounding, and his thighs chafed on the leather saddle. Still, he looked closely at the ground and searched for hoof prints emerging from the water. There were rocky areas and he wondered if he would miss where the black had come out.

Chapter 10

As he rode, Cornelius reflected on all that had transpired. Lucy had said her father hated her. Corny didn't believe that now. Surely the stern man loved his daughter. She must have inherited the same fiery temper as she attributed to him. Why else would she have gone galloping off into the darkness by herself, but then, she always did ride recklessly.

People are more alike than they are different, he thought. *Lucy is a complicated little thing, all flashing eyes, dark hair, and liquid energy. That kiss she gave me... Still, she's too young to know what she wants. Certainly not me. She did save my life and I'll do anything for her.*

The ground turned to boulders piled in disarray, and it was difficult to maneuver the dun around them. Then the trail became solid rock, and there was a cliff that dropped more than ten feet. The dun stopped and neighed. Cornelius dismounted and held the reins. He walked over and peered down. At the bottom lay the black horse on its side. Under it, with her upper body exposed, lay Lucy. Both horse and girl appeared dead.

The young man looked down and gasped with fear.

Looping the reins around a boulder, Cornelius pulled his pistol, pointed it in the air, and fired three times. Then he holstered the revolver, grabbed a canteen from the pommel of the saddle, and climbed down as quickly as he could. He walked up to the horse and saw its neck twisted at an abrupt angle. Lucy lay on the far side. Cornelius walked around and knelt down until his head was nearly touching the girl's cheek. There was still color in it. He put his hand around the back of her head and felt slippery blood. When he touched her, she groaned and opened her eyes.

"Water," she whispered.

"Thank God, you're alive," exclaimed the boy—his voice almost a sob.

Cornelius opened the canteen and gave her a drink. Some of it spilled and ran down her cheeks."

"More," she whispered again.

"Not too much," the young man answered.

She swallowed, coughed, and winced in pain.

"Poor Blacky," she cried. "I killed him."

"Shhhh," whispered Cornelius. "Lucy, you must stay calm. Wesley is on his way, and Sandy and your father are coming in the wagon."

"Father?" said the girl wonderingly, and then closed her eyes.

"Lucy? Lucy, talk to me!"

"It's all right, Corny. I'm not dead, yet."

"Lucy! Don't you even say such a thing!"

"Poor Blacky! Poor Daddy! Poor Corny! Everybody mad at me. Blacky didn't like it when I kept spurring him on."

"Lucy, think about something else."

"Did you think I was terrible, Corny? I mean when I kissed you and left?"

"No, Lucy!"

"I didn't know what you thought. I wanted you to know how I

felt. Do you think I'm some spoiled brat with a bad temper?"

"Not at all."

"Then what do you think?" demanded the girl.

"I think you're grand."

"I'm afraid I'm all busted up inside, Corny. And, and…I can't feel my legs."

"You have a twelve-hundred pound horse on you. That's why you can't feel them."

"How am I going to get out of this one, Corny?"

"We have to wait for Wesley, I can't move the horse by myself."

"Not that. I mean with Father. We had a terrible argument last night."

"I know, he told us. He doesn't care about that now. He said that he loves you and all he wants is you back—and safe."

"Did Father really say that?"

"Yes, Lucy."

The girl turned her face away and closed her eyes. Corny dabbed with the back of his hand at a tear sliding down her cheek.

"And how do you feel about me?" she asked without opening her eyes.

"I care about you very much. Now you just hold on. Wesley will be here any minute. You'll be fine. While we're waiting, tell me what you were doing way out here?

"I guess I was so angry I went clear out of my head. All I could think of was to get away."

"You certainly did that."

"Corny, if I die, will you promise not to forget about me?"

"You aren't going to die!"

"Answer the question."

"Yes, Lucy. I promise."

"Corny, I want to know what you really think of me? Tell the truth now."

"I think…"

"Yes?"

"I think, you're all fire and ice."

"Is that a good thing?"

"You bet it is," replied Corny.

"Good. Then if I live, will you promise to be my friend forever?"

"Of course."

"Then I'll try my best not to die."

Lucy turned her head back slowly and opened her eyes, her breathing was shallow and raspy.

"It hurts so much Corny, and I'm not sure I can…" Lucy's voice softened. "Will you kiss me? Show me you care?"

Corny stared at her. In her condition he was not going to argue. He bent down and did as she asked.

"No, not on my cheek. On my lips."

This time with gentle affection, he again bent down and did as she asked.

"Now you just hold on, Lucy."

"Could I have some more water? I'm still awful thirsty."

Cornelius was holding Lucy's hand when Wesley arrived. The older man climbed down, and looked at her. She was unconscious now and her pulse was weak. Both men made eye contact and there was no other sound except for the gurgling of the river and the rushing of the wind.

"Her pulse is very faint. Until we get this horse off of her, I can't tell how badly hurt she is."

Wesley climbed up, took a rope from the dun and threw one end to Cornelius. The young man put the loop around the neck of the dead horse. Then Wesley tied the rope to the pommels on the saddles of the two mounts.

"When I pull up on the horse, you take hold of Lucy and try to slide her out."

The two horses, pulling in tandem, were able to lift the heavy black enough so that Corny, with some effort, was able to pull Lucy free. Wesley climbed back down and examined her closely.

"She's breathing easier now."

Lucy's eyelids fluttered and then opened.

"My legs, they burn."

"That's a good sign, Lucy," said Wesley still kneeling at her side. "The blood is going back into them. What else hurts?"

"My left side. Something's wrong with my side and my left arm. And my head."

"Well, Lucy. You're a lucky girl."

"I don't feel lucky."

Wesley Mauldin attended to her wounds. Much later they heard the bouncing of a wagon. High up, a red-tailed hawk screamed as it glided through the blue sky. It flew over the river and ignored the moving objects in the rocks below.

"Lucy!" shouted her father as he climbed swiftly down the cliff.

"Please don't yell at me, Father," whispered Lucy.

"Thank heavens, you're alive. Daughter, I promise I won't ever yell at you again."

"Do you mean that?"

"Yes, I certainly do."

"Oh, Daddy, I killed Blacky," sobbed the girl.

"I know, honey, I'm so sorry—but the most important thing is that you're alive. I don't know what I would do if something happened to you."

The big man turned to Wesley.

"Mr. Mauldin, will she be alright?"

"She has a broken arm, some cracked ribs, and a nasty cut on her head, but I think after a few weeks, she'll be just fine."

By using rope and a board, they lifted Lucy up the cliff and placed her in the wagon. Then they wrapped her in a warm blanket.

Claude LaBarge climbed into the wagon and held his daughter's hand. Turning to Wesley and Cornelius he said, "I'm so grateful. If there is anything I can do for you, just name it."

"Well," smiled Wesley. "That's mighty nice of you, Mr. LaBarge. Now that you mention it, there is a pressing family matter you could help young Cornelius with."

Sandy, Wesley, Cornelius, and Lucy, looked to the stern visage of the older man and waited for his response

"You name it," stated LaBarge. "If it's within reason, I'll do it."

Lucy, flat on her back in the wagon, sighed heavily and then she winced in pain.

Her father, Cornelius, Sandy, and Wesley looked down at the injured girl. She beamed back at their concerned faces and gave a sigh of immense relief.

"See, Corny," she said. "Dad isn't such a bad person, once you get to know him."

Dear Reader,

If you enjoyed reading *Cornelius Goes West*, please help promote it by composing and posting a review on Amazon.com. Charlie Steel may be contacted at cowboytales@juno.com or by writing to him at the following address:

Charlie Steel
c/o Condor Publishing, Inc.
PO Box 39
Lincoln, Michigan 48742

Warm greetings from Condor Publishing, Inc.
Gail Heath, publisher

www.ingramcontent.com/pod-product-compliance
Lightning Source LLC
Chambersburg PA
CBHW030415310726
48979CB00002B/422

* 9 7 8 1 9 3 1 0 7 9 3 5 8 *